The Littles

The Littles

by **JOHN PETERSON**
Pictures by **ROBERTA CARTER CLARK**

SCHOLASTIC INC.
New York Toronto London Auckland Sydney

There are more books about the Littles
you may want to read:

All Littles books are published in paperback
by Scholastic.

ISBN 0-590-40104-1

12 11 10 9 8 7 6 5 4 3 2 1   1   6 7 8 9/8 0 1/9

Printed in the U.S.A.

To Holly

WILLIAM T. LITTLE and his family were tiny people. They lived in a house owned by George W. Bigg. Mr. Bigg and his family didn't know the Littles were living with them. The Littles kept out of sight. They lived in tiny rooms in the walls of the house.

The Littles looked almost like people you see every day. But they were very much smaller. Mr. Little was only six inches tall. And he was big for a Little. The other Littles were even smaller.

In one way the Littles did not look at all like other people. They had tails. The Littles were proud of their tails. They kept them combed and brushed, and sometimes the women curled their tails when they wanted to look especially nice.

The Littles took everything they needed from the Biggs. Usually the Biggs didn't even know anything was missing. But once in a while Mrs. Bigg would say, "Now where did that thing go? I had it right here a minute ago. It seems to have disappeared." Only last week her son Henry had shouted, "Hey, Ma! Where are my red socks? I can't find them anywhere."

And of course the Littles got all their food from the Biggs. When the Biggs had roast beef for dinner, the Littles had roast beef for dinner too.

The Biggs didn't know it, but the electric socket on the kitchen counter was a secret door. As soon as the Bigg family were busy eating their cake or pie or Jello, the Littles would dash through the door. They would take what they needed of the left-over dinner scraps and be back through the door in seconds.

The Littles helped the Biggs in return for the things they took. Only the Biggs didn't

know it. For one thing, the Littles were good at fixing things. They ran back and forth inside the walls repairing the electric wires whenever they needed it.

The Littles were good plumbers, too. On cold winter days they kept the outside water pipes from freezing. Often they had to stay up all night keeping the pipes warm by candle fire.

Mr. Bigg could never understand why his plumbing and electricity worked so well. "I can't believe it," he would say. "I have less trouble with this old house than my neighbors do with their brand-new houses." He would shake his head. "I guess they don't make houses the way they used to."

ONE day in May, the Littles were together in their living room. The two children, Tom, ten years old, and Lucy, eight, were on the sofa next to their mother.

Granny Little sat in her rocking chair knitting a red sweater for Tom. "Don't know why Henry Bigg made such a fuss when we took his old red socks," she said. "One of them had a real bad hole in the toe."

Uncle Pete, holding his cane, leaned against the fireplace. "You have enough red yarn there, Granny," he said, "to start a knitting factory."

Mr. Little was walking back and forth. "Please sit down, Will," said Mrs. Little. "You're making me nervous."

"Now there's no reason for us to be worried," said Mr. Little. "The Biggs have gone on vacation before."

"But never for three months," said Mrs. Little.

"And what about this new family?" said Uncle Pete. "The Newcombs!" He shook his cane in the air. "We don't even know them."

"We don't have to, Uncle Pete. I keep

telling you that," said Mr. Little. "If they're good enough for the Biggs, they're good enough for the Littles. Besides — they'll only be here for three months. We can stand anything for three months."

"Why do they want to rent the house for only three months?" said Tom. "Isn't that kind of silly?"

"The Newcombs are from the city," said Mr. Little. "Sometimes city people rent houses in the country while the owners are away on vacation."

"It's like a vacation for city people to live in the country for a while," said Mrs. Little.

"I don't like it," said Uncle Pete. "Suppose they bring a cat with them?"

Lucy Little moved closer to her mother. "Oh, Mother! Suppose they bring a cat with them?"

Mrs. Little put her arm around her daughter.

Granny Little stopped rocking. "Did he say they have a cat?" She nodded toward Uncle Pete.

"No, no," said Mr. Little. "He said *suppose* they had a cat."

"Oh," said Granny Little. She started rocking again. "I hope they don't bring a cat."

"Aw — who's afraid of an old cat?" said Tom.

"I wish everybody would stop talking about cats," said Lucy. "*I'm* afraid of cats." She looked from person to person. "Please, let's stop talking about cats."

THERE was a secret look-out place behind the light switch in the hall of the Biggs' house. One of the screws was missing. The empty hole was large enough for a Little to look and listen through.

Mr. Little spent all the next day at the look-out place. Tom Little stayed with him. They were waiting for the Newcombs.

"When they come, be careful of that light switch, Tom," said Mr. Little. "Likely as not, the first thing they'll do is turn on the hall light."

Sometime in the late afternoon, Mr. Little thought he heard a noise. He looked through the hole.

"Are they coming?" said Tom.

"Not yet . . . hold it!" Mr. Little heard a key in the front door lock. "Yes — here they come now — sh!"

"Where's the hall light, Charlie?" It was a woman's voice.

"I have it," said Charles Newcomb.

There were sparks inside the look-out
place as the light was turned on. Tom Little
jumped. His father turned from the peep-hole
and put his finger to his lips. "Sh!" The bright
light from the hall came through the peep-hole
into their dark hiding place. Tom could see
his father's face clearly. Mr. Little returned to
the hole.

"What a drive!" said Mrs. Newcomb. She sat down heavily on the suitcase. "Give me a minute to rest and I'll help you with the rest of the bags."

"No need to help, Mrs. N.," said Mr. Newcomb. "I'll get the bags myself. No tipping, please. It's part of the service here at the Biggs' Summer Hotel."

Mrs. Newcomb laughed. "Where do you get the energy?" she said.

"From the country!" said Mr. Newcomb. "I didn't realize how much I'd missed it. I get energy from just looking at all the trees and space. We're going to be here *three* months. Think of it!"

"I am," said Mrs. Newcomb. "I'll still have to get three meals a day — only now it'll be in a strange kitchen."

"Listen, Liz," said Mr. Newcomb. "You've

come here to write. And I've come here to paint. Nothing else is important."

"Sure, sure!" Mrs. Newcomb laughed. "Tell me that after eating hamburger for a week."

"I mean it, Liz," said Mr. Newcomb. "Forget about housework. Write those stories you want to write. As for me —" He twirled around and did a little dance. "This isn't my house. I'm fixing nothing and I'm doing nothing. If the faucets drip, let 'em drip! I may not even take out the garbage."

"You really mean it, don't you?" said Mrs. Newcomb.

"Sure I do!" said Mr. Newcomb. "I'm here to paint masterpieces, and that's what I'm going to do. And when I'm not doing that, I'm going to do nothing! I'll loaf! Sit in the sun and eat!" He laughed. "Hamburgers, of course."

A WEEK had passed. Uncle Pete thought it was a bad beginning. "It looks as though Newcomb means what he says. The place is a mess since they came." He pushed his plate away and threw down his napkin. "And I *am* getting tired of hamburger."

"No matter," said Mr. Little. "It'll be over one day, and the Biggs will return. No harm done."

"Something bad will come of it, you'll see," said Uncle Pete.

"Well, at least they don't have a cat," said Lucy Little.

"That's right," said Mrs. Little. She smiled at her family. "Lucy is looking on the bright side. Things could be worse."

"Bah!" said Uncle Pete. "Right now I'd rather have trouble with a cat than eat this cooking."

"I suppose I should have learned to cook," said Mrs. Little. She looked around the table. "Mrs. Bigg was such a good cook it didn't seem necessary for me to cook too. I guess she spoiled us."

All the Littles nodded.

Suddenly Granny Little spoke, "Watch out for mice."

"Why do you say that, Granny?" said Mr. Little. "There are no mice in this house. George Bigg wouldn't stand for it."

Granny Little looked sharply at Mr. Little. "There will be mice," she said. Then she straightened the shawl on her shoulders.

"Don't worry, Granny," said Mr. Little. "You're thinking of the old days. This is nothing like the old days."

ALL day Mrs. Newcomb worked hard at her writing. In the evening, after dinner, she read what she had written to Mr. Newcomb. They sat in the living room. Sometimes Mr. Newcomb drew pictures of his wife while she was reading.

The Littles became interested in the story. They would rush through their dinner, so they wouldn't miss anything.

The Littles' living room was in the wall next to the Biggs' living room, near the ceiling. There was a hole in the wall between the Littles' living room and the Biggs' living room. The hole was about the size of a quarter. On the Biggs' side it was covered with wallpaper. Mr. Little had punched many tiny holes in the wallpaper. He used one of Mrs. Bigg's needles.

Voices could be heard through the tiny holes. Most of the time the hole was plugged up with a cork on the Littles' side. As long as the cork was in the hole, no one could hear the Littles. When the cork was taken out, the Littles would be very quiet and listen.

The cork was always out when it was story time. Mrs. Newcomb's soft voice would float up through the hole. The Littles sat comfortably in their favorite chairs and listened.

Sometimes Mrs. Newcomb read until it was past Lucy's and Tom's bedtime. They would beg their mother to be allowed to stay up until the story was finished.

Even Uncle Pete liked the readings. "Wonderful story," he said. "Very exciting!" Still, he wasn't happy with the Newcombs. "The bad housekeeping — it worries me."

The Newcombs were indeed bad house-keepers. Food was left around uncovered. Floors were not swept after meals. Garbage spilled out of the can. When the lid fell off, it wasn't put back on.

"All those crumbs! Mark my words," Granny said, "there WILL be mice."

One day in June Mr. Little rushed into the living room. He slammed the door behind him. "Granny was right," he said. "I've been hoping it wouldn't happen — but it has! They've come! The mice are here!"

"What can we do?" said Mrs. Little. She locked the door behind her husband.

"First — you, Tom — see that all the doors are locked!" said Mr. Little. Tom ran to do as he was told.

Mr. Little went quickly to the sofa. He pulled a chest out from under it. "Don't go out alone," he said. "Go armed at all times." Mr. Little opened the chest. He looked up at his wife. "Who would think that this generation of Littles would have to open this weapons chest?"

Mrs. Little shook her head sadly.

"But, Father," said Lucy. "I don't know how to use a bow and arrow."

"Uncle Pete will teach you and Tom how to shoot," said Mr. Little. "He was a crack shot during the Mice Invasion of '35. Uncle Pete, my father, and their brothers held off the mice from this very room until help arrived from the Smalls down the road."

"That's when I got this limp," said Uncle Pete. "A huge three-inch mouse broke through the door and grabbed me by the foot. He dragged me out of the room. My brother Tim, God bless him, came after me and shot him."

"Is that when Uncle Tim lost his life?" said Tom.

"That's when it happened," said Uncle Pete. "One of those big mice jumped him from behind. I finally chased it off with my knife, but it was too late." Uncle Pete wiped his eyes. "Poor Tim. He was the only Little we lost in that terrible year."

"We won't go looking for trouble with the mice," said Mr. Little. "These weapons are for protection only." He brought out a bow with a quiver of arrows from the chest. On the wooden bow was carved, *"Made in 1825 by Chas. B. Little."*

"Suppose they come after us," said Tom. He picked up the bow and tried to put the string on it.

"Maybe they won't," said Mr. Little, "as long as there's plenty to eat."

"I'm for going out and attacking them," said Uncle Pete. "Teach 'em a lesson *before* they start to bother us."

"The way I figure it," said Mr. Little, "after a while the Newcombs are bound to find out they have mice. When they do, they'll set traps, and that'll be the end of it."

EVERY night for a week Mr. Little and Tom watched the Newcombs at dinner time. Mr. Little wanted to find out if the Newcombs had seen the mice — and what, if anything, they were doing to get rid of them. Tom and his father hid high above the dinner table in a secret look-out place near the ceiling light. They could see everything that went on in the room.

Below them, the Newcombs were finishing their dinner. "I saw a hummingbird outside the study window today," said Mrs. Newcomb. "It was feeding on the iris."

"Marvelous!" said Mr. Newcomb. "Would you mind passing the butter? That's a rare thing to see, you know — they're so tiny and timid."

"And fast!" said Mrs. Newcomb, "I moved closer to the window for a better look, and it was gone in a flash."

Mr. Newcomb sipped his coffee. "Mmm. Dear, don't you think this coffee is a bit weak again?"

Mrs. Newcomb nodded. "What's the bird that sounds like a rusty iron gate?"

Above them, the Littles listened. The Newcombs talked about many things. But as

usual neither one said anything about the mice. "Let's go," said Mr. Little to Tom. "They haven't seen the mice."

Father and son climbed out of the lookout place. They walked across the ceiling between the rafters. Both were armed. Tom was carrying a bow and a quiver full of arrows. Mr. Little had a sword. He was carrying a lighted candle.

"What can we do?" said Tom. "The Newcombs see birds everywhere *outside* the house. But *inside*, where the mice are, they never see anything! Are they blind or something?"

Mr. Little sighed. "I don't know," he said. "Mice are quick animals. They're not easy to see. And they usually do most of their work when people are not around."

"Hey! I have an idea," said Tom Little. "I know how we can get them to see the mice."

"How?"

"It's easy. We can . . ."

Just then Tom's father stopped. Tom, following close behind, bumped into him. The candle fell from Mr. Little's hand and went out. Mr. Little reached for his sword.

"Is it a mouse?" whispered Tom.

"Sh!"

Quietly, Tom took an arrow and fitted it to the bow string.

There was a scratching noise in the wall ahead. Mr. Little and Tom stood still and tried to see into the blackness. They listened.

When Mr. Little had heard enough to know it was a mouse, he whispered to Tom, "I'll stand here. You hide behind that heating pipe. As soon as the mouse reaches the top of the wall, I'll light a match." He took a deep breath. "If he runs to attack me, shoot him with your bow and arrow. Don't shoot unless he attacks. The light may frighten him away."

"What if I miss?" said Tom.

"I have the sword," said Mr. Little.

"The mouse will have to get awfully close for you to use the sword," said Tom.

"That's why you'd better not miss with the arrow," said Mr. Little. "Now go!"

Tom Little felt his way through the dark ceiling space to the pipe. He drew the arrow across the bow and pulled the string back with all his might. Then he aimed into the darkness toward the sound of the scratching.

The noise grew louder and louder. From the sound of it, Tom thought the mouse was climbing near the Littles' tin-can elevator. He hoped the mouse hadn't gnawed through the string.

The boy had never seen a mouse. He had,

of course, heard many scary stories about them. He was ready for something terrible.

Suddenly there was a burst of blinding white light. His father's match! Shadows danced. Tom Little blinked.

Then he saw the mouse.

It was climbing up over the edge of the wall. Its eyes were like black mirrors, shining back the light of the match. Tom forgot what his father had told him. He didn't wait for the mouse to attack. Instead, as soon as he saw the beast, he shot the arrow. It flew through the air and struck the mouse in the foreleg. The mouse squealed.

"Nuts!" yelled Tom. "I forgot!" He shot another arrow. By that time the mouse had climbed over the wall. As it struggled to its feet, the second arrow hit it in the rump. It squealed louder.

The arrows didn't stop the mouse. It crawled toward the light. A low, snarling growl came from deep in its throat.

Mr. Little stood his ground in the middle of the ceiling space four feet away from the oncoming mouse. In one hand he held the sword at arm's length, pointed at the mouse. In the other he held the burning match high over his head like a torch. Then he lowered the match-torch and pointed it at the mouse.

Suddenly the mouse turned and limped away.

MR. LITTLE and Tom were not the only Littles who fought with mice that day. Uncle Pete and Lucy had a narrow escape in the cellar.

They had been burning trash at the hot-water heater when two mice trapped them. Uncle Pete and Lucy were under the water tank next to the burner, and there was no safe way out.

At first Uncle Pete tried to fight them off with his bow and arrows. But the old bow string broke with the first shot, and he missed.

Luckily, Uncle Pete had made two torches from burnt matches he found near the heater. He had wrapped rags around the ends of the match sticks. Then he dipped them in a puddle of oil near the furnace.

When the bow string broke, Uncle Pete lit the torches. He and Lucy waved them at the mice and frightened them away.

Back in the safety of their rooms, Uncle Pete made a new bow string. He waxed it carefully and strung it on the bow.

"Someone's going to get hurt if this keeps up," said Mrs. Little. "When are the Newcombs going to help us?"

"Probably never!" said Uncle Pete.

"Tom has a plan," said Mr. Little. "It's a good plan, and I think it will work. Tell your idea, Tom."

"Well," said Tom. "Those Newcombs never see the mice, so they don't bother to set traps — right?"

Tom's mother nodded.

"Suppose we show them a mouse. Then they'll know — right?"

"How do we do *that?*" said Uncle Pete. "We don't have any mice. Your mouse got away and my bow string broke."

"We don't want them to see a dead mouse anyway," said Mr. Little.

"Then what on earth is the boy talking about?" said Uncle Pete. "Get to the point!"

"Suppose I dressed up like a mouse," said Tom. "I could run across the kitchen floor right in front of Mrs. Newcomb."

"Good heavens!" said Uncle Pete. "Is the woman an idiot? Couldn't she tell a fake mouse from a real one?"

"If the fake mouse went fast enough," said Mrs. Little, "she might think it was real."

"There's only one thing wrong with Tom's plan," said Mr. Little. "*I'll* do the mouse running. As head of the family, it's my job."

"But, Dad — you're too big!" said Tom. "I'm just the right size. It won't look right if you do it."

"Oh dear," said Mrs. Little. "Do you think so?"

"The boy's right," said Uncle Pete. "If we're going to use his plan, let's do it right. He's the perfect size for the job."

It was decided. Tom would play the part of the mouse. Mr. Little would go with him to tell him when and where to run. Granny Little set to work making the costume.

By the next afternoon they were ready. Tom was dressed in the costume. He looked quite a bit like a real mouse, even from close up. Granny Little had done her work well. She had sewed on ears and whiskers. Tom used his own tail, of course. His mother oiled and brushed down the hair so it had the shape of a mouse's tail.

"Tom, you look a fright," said Mr. Little.

Uncle Pete came into the room. "Mrs. Newcomb's in the kitchen now," he said. "It's time you two got moving."

"Just a minute, just a minute," said Granny Little. She was on her knees making some last-minute changes. "It's too loose around the ankles. You don't want him to trip, do you?"

Lucy stood behind her mother sneaking looks at Tom. "Mother, doesn't he look *awful?*" she said.

"I want to see myself in the mirror." said Tom.

"Hold still, hold still," said Granny Little. She worked for a moment longer. "There!" She stood up and looked at her work.

"Granny, it's wonderful!" said Mrs. Little.

"It's awful!" said Lucy.

The family followed Tom as he squeaked and galloped on all fours over to the mirror.

"Tom," said Mr. Little. "This is not a joke. I want you to remember that."

"I'm practicing," said Tom.

"The boy is high-spirited, that's all," said Uncle Pete. "I was that way myself when I was his age."

Mr. Little had to pull his son away from the mirror. "Come, Tom," he said. "We're wasting time. Mrs. Newcomb may not be in the kitchen for long."

All the Littles went with Mr. Little and Tom down the passageway as far as the tin-can elevator. Mrs. Little tried to kiss Tom, but the mouse costume covered his head. Instead she pulled his tail gently. "Be careful, Tom. Do just as your father tells you," she said.

"He'll be all right," said Mr. Little. "He knows what to do. We've gone over it and over it."

"What's all the fuss?" said Uncle Pete. "They'll be back shortly."

Mr. Little and Tom climbed into the tin can. They had rigged up the tin-can elevator from an old soup can and bits of string tied together. The elevator dropped slowly out of sight.

"It's the first time any of the big people have *ever* seen any of us," said Mrs. Little. "And the only real part of Tom they'll see is his tail."

Down in the kitchen, Mr. Little hid behind a waste basket. He got ready to give Tom the signal to go.

The tiny man held up his hand, waiting for the right moment. If Mrs. Newcomb was too close, she might step on Tom. But if she weren't facing the right way, she might not see Tom run across the floor.

Mr. Little waited. Tom watched his father carefully.

Mrs. Newcomb turned toward the waste basket, where Mr. Little was hiding.

Mr. Little's hand dropped.

Just then Mrs. Newcomb started walking.

"No, Tom! Wait!" whispered Mr. Little.

Too late! Tom Little came skittering across the kitchen floor just in time to run between Mrs. Newcomb's feet.

Mr. Little closed his eyes.

"EEEEEEEeeeeeee!" shouted Mrs. Newcomb. "A mouse!"

Mr. Little opened his eyes. Tom was safe under the radiator on the other side of the room.

"CHARLIE!" shouted Mrs. Newcomb. "THERE'S A MOUSE IN THE KITCHEN!"

Mr. Newcomb came running.

"This house has mice!" said Mrs. Newcomb. "One of them almost jumped on me!"

"Take it easy, Liz," said Mr. Newcomb. He got down on his knees and looked around.

"Charlie, you *must* get rid of the mice," said Mrs. Newcomb. "I won't live in a house with mice."

"We'll get rid of them," said Mr. Newcomb. "The Biggs must have mouse traps around someplace. Just don't get so excited, Liz. It's only a little mouse."

"Don't get excited, you say," said Mrs. Newcomb. "You should have seen it. It ran straight at me! It might have bitten me, it came so close."

"You think a mouse would *bite* you?" said Mr. Newcomb.

"You can't tell," said Mrs. Newcomb. "You never can tell what a wild animal like that will do."

THE LITTLES were very pleased with the success of Tom's plan. Mr. Little couldn't get over it. "I wish you all could have seen Tom," he said. "Zip, he went — right across the floor. 'It's a mouse!' yelled Mrs. Newcomb. Oh my! It was something to see."

"He's a Little all right," said Uncle Pete. "He has that Little bravery."

"I only had a *little* bravery is right, Uncle Pete," said Tom. "I was kind of scared."

All the Littles laughed except Uncle Pete.

"Tom Little, you ripped this mouse costume," said Granny Little. She was looking at it under a light.

"I'm sorry, Granny," said Tom. "I was going so fast I couldn't stop when I got to the other side of the room. I tore it on a nail under the radiator."

"I'll fix it," said Granny Little. "You can wear it next Halloween."

"I hate mice," said Lucy. "Don't wear that thing ever again, please."

"Granny, you did a wonderful job on the costume," said Mr. Little. "But . . . well, no one really likes it. Do you know what I mean?"

"No sense in wasting all that good work," said Granny Little. She started sewing. "We may need it again."

"I'm not leaving my room until the mice are gone," said Lucy.

"They'll be gone in a few days," said Mr. Little. "You'll see. Everything is going to be all right now."

"I say we should give Newcomb a helping hand," said Uncle Pete. He picked up a sword made from one of Mrs. Bigg's needles. "On guard!" Uncle Pete limped forward, waving the sword and stabbing the air. "Take that! And that!"

"Oh goodness, Uncle Pete — do put that thing down," said Mrs. Little. "I hate to see those weapons around." She turned to her husband. "When can we put them back in the chest?"

"As soon as the mice are gone," said Mr. Little. "I figure a few days at the most. In the meantime I want all of you to watch out for the mouse traps. We don't want any accidents now that our troubles are almost over."

"Why don't we stay in our rooms for the next few days?" said Mrs. Little. "Then we'll be safe from the traps *and* the mice."

Uncle Pete didn't think so. "We should know what's going on at all times," he said. "Bad business — sticking your head in the sand like an ostrich."

"Let's look around once a day, then," said Mr. Little. "That should be enough."

"I'm going down to the kitchen first thing tomorrow morning," said Uncle Pete. "I want to see those mouse traps with my own eyes."

"May I go with Uncle Pete this time?" said Tom. "Lucy doesn't want to go, do you, Lucy?"

"I'm not leaving my room until the mice are gone," said Lucy Little for the second time.

THE next morning Mr. Little was walking
back and forth in the Littles' kitchen. Mrs.
Little and Lucy sat at a table watching him.
Granny Little was sitting at the table too,
knitting. Mr. Little kept looking up at the clock
on the wall. "Ten o'clock," he said, "and they're
not here. They should have come back a half
an hour ago."

"Who's not here?" said Granny Little.

"Uncle Pete and Tom," said Mr. Little. "They went to the kitchen to see if the mouse traps had been set."

"What shall we do?" said Mrs. Little.

Mr. Little strapped on his sword. "I'm going to find them," he said. "They're probably all right, but I can't stand the waiting."

"I'd better go with you," said Mrs. Little.

"No, I can handle it alone," said Mr. Little. "I want you here with Granny, just in case."

"Do you think mice would come here?"

"No, but you can't be sure," said Mr. Little. "They did in '35. When there are enough of them, they'll try anything."

When Mr. Little got to the kitchen, he couldn't find Uncle Pete and Tom. He didn't see any mouse traps either.

He went to the cellar. Still no sign of the boy and his uncle. And there were no mouse traps in the cellar. "Something's wrong," thought Mr. Little.

Mr. Little went to the garbage can. There *had* to be mouse traps there. It was the best place to catch mice. But there were none. And still no sign of the missing Littles.

"It's very strange," thought Mr. Little. "No mice, no mouse traps, and no Tom or Uncle Pete." He decided to return to the kitchen. That's where Uncle Pete wanted to go in the first place. So Mr. Little turned back and headed for the kitchen.

Meanwhile, back in the Littles' rooms, Lucy was thinking about her father. "Suppose he needs someone to send a message or something. I should have gone with him."

She looked into the living room. Granny Little was sitting in her chair by the fireplace. Lucy's mother was watching the door, a kitchen knife in her lap.

"I should be with my father," thought Lucy. Then suddenly she made up her mind. She ran to her room and got the bow and arrows. Then she slipped out the back door into the passageway.

Mr. Little was in the kitchen under the radiator. He waited until he could hear the Newcombs talking in the living room. Then he felt it was safe to look around.

Near the door to the dining room he came upon Uncle Pete's sword. "Uncle Pete would never let go of his sword," he thought, "unless it was knocked from his hands. This is bad. I wonder if..." He put the thought out of his mind. "Don't think," he told himself. "Just keep looking."

Mr. Little drew his sword. He went into the dining room. He kept close to the wall and walked slowly toward the fireplace.

Just as Mr. Little was leaving the kitchen, Lucy got there. She saw her father go into the dining room, sword in hand. Lucy ran to catch up. Her father was only a few feet ahead of her when, suddenly—a giant cat leaped at him out of the shadows!

Lucy was never so scared in her life. She ran toward the cat. She ran without thinking. The gigantic animal had attacked her father. She would save her father somehow.

The tiny girl came up behind the cat. Its
long tail swished back and forth over her head.
She took an arrow and jabbed it as hard as
she could into the cat's tail.

"EEEEeeeooooowww!" yelled the cat. And it ran out of the dining room, through the hall, and into the living room.

Mr. Little was not hurt. He jumped to his feet. At the same time, Uncle Pete and Tom came running out of the fireplace. They had been cornered by the cat and were hiding under the logs.

"Let's get out of here!" yelled Mr. Little. He ran for the kitchen.

"Not without this," said Uncle Pete. He bent down and scooped up his sword.

The four Littles dashed under the radiator and through the trap door.

MRS. LITTLE and Granny Little were still in the living room when the other Littles hurried in.

"Lucy!" said Mrs. Little. "I thought you were in your room. What happened, Will? Why is Lucy with you?"

Mr. Little told his wife what had happened. "Lucky for us Lucy decided to follow me when she did," he said. "I still can't believe it. She attacked that huge cat." He shook his head.

"It's amazing!" said Uncle Pete. "Absolutely amazing!"

"We were pinned under the logs, Mother," said Tom. "I never got a chance to shoot my bow and arrows."

"What are we going to do about that cat?" said Uncle Pete. "Never thought they'd get a cat to chase the mice."

"We're safe inside the walls at least," said Mr. Little. "That monster won't be able to get us here."

"There's the problem of getting supplies," said Uncle Pete. "We'll have to leave the walls for that."

"I think I know how we can get rid of the cat," said Mr. Little.

"How?" said all the Littles.

"By getting it in trouble," said Mr. Little. "We can pull down the curtains for one thing — the Newcombs will blame it on the cat. We can keep spilling its milk. At night we can make loud cat noises to keep the Newcombs awake. We can even knock over lamps so they will think the cat did it. Pretty soon the Newcombs will think they have the wrong kind of cat. They'll want to get rid of it."

Everybody agreed that Mr. Little's plan was a good one. During the next few weeks the Newcombs came to believe their cat was clumsy and noisy.

One day the cat seemed to knock over a lamp. Another time the Newcombs were awake half the night listening to meowing. It was really the Littles making a terrible racket. The day after that the curtains in the dining room were pulled down.

"What do we do tomorrow, Dad?" said Tom. "May I spill the cat's milk?"

"That's good—yes," said Mr. Little. "It should be done two or three times in a row, though. Then Mrs. Newcomb will get awfully tired of cleaning it up."

"There's only one thing wrong with this plan, Will," said Mrs. Little.

"I don't know why you say that," said Mr. Little. "Everything has worked perfectly so far. What's wrong with the plan?"

"The cat is still in the house," said Mrs. Little.

"Don't worry," said Mr. Little. "It won't be here long."

"Mrs. Newcomb must be mad as a wet hen by now," said Uncle Pete.

The next day Tom had a close call. Just as he was lifting the cat's milk dish to spill it for the third time, the cat showed up. The huge animal came bounding toward Tom. At the last moment Tom upset the milk dish under the cat's nose. That stopped the cat long enough for Tom to get away.

"This plan of yours is too slow, Will," said Uncle Pete. "We're going to have to do something else before that cat gets one of us."

"What can we do?" said Mr. Little.

"We need larger weapons," said Uncle Pete.

"I don't know if that's the answer, Uncle Pete," said Mr. Little. "Besides, that takes time too. You're right, though — this plan isn't working. I heard Mrs. Newcomb telling Mr. Newcomb not to get rid of the cat. She's afraid the mice will return.

"And she *likes* the cat," Mr. Little went on. "Thinks it's cute. She says it's high-spirited."

"Not only that," said Mrs. Little, "We can't break up everything in the house just to get rid of the cat. It's the Biggs' house, after all."

"Why don't we try taming the cat?" said Tom.

"What?" said Uncle Pete.

"Let's see if we can tame it," repeated Tom. "Cats have been friends to men since the early days of history."

Uncle Pete looked from Mrs. Little to Mr. Little. "Do you hear what the boy is saying?" he said. "He's gone soft in the head."

"No kidding, Dad," said Tom. "It's true. The early Egyptians thought cats were gods. They had them all over the place."

"They did, did they?" said Uncle Pete. "Where did you hear such nonsense?"

"I read it in one of the Biggs' history books," said Tom.

Uncle Pete snorted. "A cat has never been a friend to a Little. I can tell you that."

"Maybe that's because none of them ever tried to tame a cat," said Tom. "They were always *afraid* of cats."

"What kind of silly talk is that, boy?" said Uncle Pete. "Look at the size of the beast. Who could tame such a monster?"

"Men tame elephants," said Tom.

"Tom has an interesting idea," said Mr. Little. "Perhaps we're worried too much about the size of the cat. Because we're so small we've always thought *all* large animals were our enemies. Maybe that's wrong."

"I don't like the way this talk is going," said Uncle Pete. "It's against everything we Littles believe. Making friends with a cat is like making friends with a rattlesnake."

"Tom is saying it's *not* the same thing," said Mr. Little. "Cats are friendly to men — rattlesnakes are not."

None of the Littles spoke.

"Now we may be little," said Mr. Little,

"but we *are* men."

"Of course we are," said Uncle Pete. He looked sideways at his tail. "We're not animals."

"Then why can't we have a cat around the house just like other people?"

"Of all the silly ideas!" said Uncle Pete.

"Oh dear," said Mrs. Little. "It *sounds* all right. But I don't know . . ."

"Why, it's a wonderful idea!" said Granny Little. "It's so simple."

"Simple-*minded!*" said Uncle Pete.

"Why didn't someone think of it before?" said Granny Little.

"Because it's a coo-coo idea, that's why," said Uncle Pete.

"Now see here, Peter Little," said Granny Little. "Mind your manners." She stood up. Her ball of knitting yarn fell from her lap. It rolled between Mr. Little's feet. "I've lived a few more days than you have. And I know a few more things than you do, too."

Mr. Little picked up the ball of yarn. He tossed it gently in the air a few times. "We could start taming the cat by giving her a present — show her we mean to be friendly."

"Give her something to play with," said Tom.

"How about that ball of yarn your father is fiddling with?" said Granny Little. "Don't cats like to play with things like that?"

"As a matter of fact, Granny, they do," said Mr. Little.

"Will that make her friendly?" said Mrs. Little.

"It might help," said Mr. Little. "We could roll a ball of yarn at the cat and see what happens. All we have to do is make sure we have room to get out of the way if she doesn't get the idea."

"I'm against it," said Uncle Pete. "Too dangerous. Cats are cats—you can't change 'em."

"There's a large ball of yarn in Mrs. Bigg's sewing basket." said Lucy. "I lifted it once. It's lighter than anything."

"Let's get it," said Mr. Little. "I think it's worth trying." He looked at Uncle Pete. "That is, if no one else has any better ideas."

"Count me out," said Uncle Pete. "I'll stay here and sharpen my sword."

THEY found the cat in the cellar. She was sleeping near the stairs.

Mr. and Mrs. Little and the children stood by the trap door under the stairs. They all held onto the end of the yarn. Mr. Little rolled the yarn toward the cat.

The cat opened one eye as the yarn went past her nose. Her paw shot out. She batted

the ball of yarn. The yarn rolled to a stop in front of the trap door.

"Oh dear," whispered Mrs. Little. "Will we be able to get through the trap door if we have to?"

"Don't move!" whispered Mr. Little.

The cat jumped up to run after the yarn.

When she saw the Littles, she stopped. She went into a crouch. Her eyes were hard, and her tail began twitching. The cat was getting set to attack.

Suddenly Tom walked a few steps toward the cat. He held out his hand. "Nice kitty," he said in a soft voice. "Come here, kitty."

"Tom! Pssst! Tom!" Mr. Little hissed. "Come back! Don't be foolish."

"Here, kitty, kitty," said Tom again.

The cat's tail stopped twitching. She cocked her head and looked at Tom.

"Here, kitty, kitty, kitty," Tom went on. "Come here, girl."

"Mee-ow!" said the cat. Her eyes softened.

"Amazing!" said Mr. Little under his breath.

Tom took a few more steps. "Nice kitty," he said over and over again.

Then the Littles heard a strange noise coming from the cat. A deep, soft, pleasant humming. The cat was purring.

Now Tom was standing next to the cat. He reached up and scratched her gently under the chin. The cat closed her eyes slowly and purred louder. Tom kept talking to her all the while.

"It was the talking that did it," said Mr.

Little later. "The way I figure, the cat didn't know we were people until Tom started talking to her. I guess cats like people to talk to them."

When the Newcombs left to return to the city, the cat didn't go with them. They thought she had wandered away and got lost. She hadn't. The cat had grown so fond of the Littles, she didn't want to leave. For one thing, Tom had taken to riding on the cat's back. The two became great friends. They went everywhere together.

The day the Newcombs left, the cat found a hiding place and stayed out of sight. Mr. Newcomb looked all over the house. He never found her. "It's just as well," said Mrs. Newcomb. "She wouldn't have much fun in the city."

"If she shows up, George Bigg will take care of her," said Mr. Newcomb.

The Bigg family came back from their vacation to find the cat sleeping next to the cellar stairs. "That cat must have sneaked in somehow," said Mr. Bigg. "We'll have to get rid of it."

Tom Little had other ideas. "Not if I can help it," he said. Tom knew he would be able to think up something to make Mr. Bigg change his mind. But that is probably another story.